Atsuko Morozumi

Mummy is that You?

MATHEW PRICE

Mrs Duck had four eggs
in her little house underneath
the willow tree.

One blowy day a gust of wind picked up her house and threw it high into the air.

The nest flew and flew in the wind till
it landed on someone's back,

with a PLONK!

The eggs cracked open and four
little ducklings were born.

"Hello," they said. "Are you our Mummy?"

"Certainly not," said the tortoise.

So the ducklings set off to find their Mummy. First they met someone soft and fluffy.

"Are you our Mummy?"
they asked.

"Dear me, no," growled the dog.

The ducklings left in a hurry.

The four little ducklings
were just having a rest, when
somebody walked by with lots of
little babies just like them.

"She must be Mummy," they cried.

"I'm sorry," said the hen,
"but I'm not your Mummy."

Next the ducklings came to a pond.
Someone was splashing
about in the water.
"Are you our Mummy?"
they called out.

"You must be joking," said the fish,
as she swam away.

The ducklings decided to have
a swim too.

They were happily splashing about,
when one of them swam smack into a
white, fluffy back.

"Quackety quack, what's that?"
a voice said.

A lovely duck turned around,
looking at them all with a big smile.
"Mummy!"

Mrs Duck took her ducklings home. Their little house was back in its place underneath the willow tree. This time it was tied fast with a great big rope.

The End